My First

1 2 3

Pamela Allen

Puffin Baby

1 One

One hungry crocodile.

Snap! Snap! Snap!

2 Two

Two donkeys racing.

Clippity-clop. Clippity-clop.

3 Three

Three dinosaurs stamping.

Stomp. Stomp. Stomp.

4 Four

Four boys howling.

Yow! Eeee! Owwwwww!

5 Five

Five dogs chasing.

Woof! Woof! Woof!

6 Six

Six bears dancing.

Pom. Pom. Pom.

7 Seven

Seven ducks flapping.

Quack! Quack! Quack!

8 Eight

Eight babies crying.

Waah! Waah! Waah!

9 Nine

Nine seagulls screeching.

Looka-looka-looka!

10 Ten

Ten curious cows.

Moo. Moo. Moo.

1

2

3

4

5

6

7

8

9

10

PUFFIN BABY

Published by the Penguin Group
Penguin Group (Australia)
250 Camberwell Road
Camberwell, Victoria 3124, Australia
(a division of Pearson Australia Group Pty Ltd)
Penguin Group (USA) Inc.
375 Hudson Street, New York, New York 10014, USA
Penguin Group (Canada)
90 Eglinton Avenue East, Suite 700,
Toronto ON M4P 2Y3, Canada
(a division of Pearson Penguin Canada Inc.)
Penguin Books Ltd
80 Strand, London WC2R ORL, England
Penguin Ireland
25 St Stephen's Green, Dublin 2, Ireland
(a division of Penguin Books Ltd)
Penguin Books India Pvt Ltd
11, Community Centre, Panchsheel Park, New Delhi -110 017, India
Penguin Group (NZ)
67 Apollo Drive, Rosedale, North Shore 0632, New Zealand
(a division of Pearson New Zealand Ltd)
Penguin Books (South Africa) (Pty) Ltd
24 Sturdee Avenue, Rosebank, Johannesburg 2196, South Africa

Penguin Books Ltd, Registered Offices: 80 Strand, London WC2R ORL, England

First published by Penguin Group (Australia), a division of Pearson Australia Group Pty Ltd, 2007

1 3 5 7 9 10 8 6 4 2

Copyright © Pamela Allen, 2007

The moral right of the author/illustrator has been asserted

Designed by Elizabeth Dias © Penguin Group (Australia)
Series Design by John Canty © Penguin Group (Australia)
Printed in China by Everbest Printing Co Ltd

National Library of Australia
Cataloguing-in-Publication data:

Allen, Pamela.
My first 1, 2, 3

ISBN: 978 0 14 350203 6.

1. Counting – Juvenile literature. I. Title. (Series: Puffin baby).

513.211

puffin.com.au